OTHER BOOKS YOU MAY ENJOY

The Wonder Child & Other Jewish Fairy Tales
Selected and retold by Howard Schwartz and Barbara Rush
Pictures in full color by Stephen Fieser

The Diamond Tree: Jewish Tales from Around the World
Selected and retold by Howard Schwartz and Barbara Rush
Pictures in full color by Uri Shulevitz

The Sabbath Lion: A Jewish Folktale from Algeria
Retold by Howard Schwartz and Barbara Rush
Pictures in full color by Stephen Fieser

BOOKS EDITED BY HOWARD SCHWARTZ

Elijah's Violin & Other Jewish Fairy Tales
Miriam's Tambourine: Jewish Folktales from Around the World
Lilith's Cave: Jewish Tales of the Supernatural
Gabriel's Palace: Jewish Mystical Tales

INVISIBLE KINGDOMS

Jewish Tales of Angels, Spirits, and Demons

Retold by Howard Schwartz
Pictures by Stephen Fieser

HARPERCOLLINS*PUBLISHERS*

Thanks to Antonia Markiet, my editor at HarperCollins Children's Books,

for her encouragement and support.

Thanks also to Arielle North Olson for assistance in the editing of these stories.

Invisible Kingdoms: Jewish Tales of Angels, Spirits, and Demons
Text copyright © 2002 by Howard Schwartz
Illustrations copyright © 2002 by Stephen Fieser
For information address HarperCollins Children's Books, a division of HarperCollins Publishers,
1350 Avenue of the Americas, New York, NY 10019.
www.harperchildrens.com
Library of Congress Cataloging-in-Publication Data
Schwartz, Howard, date
   Invisible Kingdoms : Jewish tales of angels, spirits, and demons / retold by Howard Schwartz ; pictures by Stephen
Fieser.
      p.   cm.
   Summary: A collection of nine tales from countries around the world, dealing with an assortment of supernatural creatures.
   ISBN 0-06-027855-2 — ISBN 0-06-027856-0 (lib. bdg.)
   1. Supernatural—Folklore.   2. Jews—Folklore.   3. Tales.   [1. Supernatural—Folklore.   2. Jews—Folklore.   3. Folklore.]
I. Fieser, Stephen, ill.   II. Title.
PZ8.1S4 In   2002   00-038901
398.2'089'924—dc21   CIP
                                                                                                    AC
Typography by Al Cetta
1   2   3   4   5   6   7   8   9   10
❖
First Edition

For Shira

Nathan

and Miriam

and for Tsila

with thanks

—H. S.

For Luis,

Edith,

And Eileen:

Cento Anni

—S. F.

Contents

Introduction

Since ancient times, Jewish storytellers have described a world with invisible creatures—angels, spirits, and demons. Angels serve as messengers of God. Spirits of the dead haunt this world as ghosts. And demons are forces of evil, capable of stealing a person's soul.

Belief in these mysterious, invisible creatures has lasted for thousands of years; even today, many people still believe in them. Angels are first found in the Bible—the three that are named are Gabriel, Michael, and the Angel of Death. Spirits are souls of the dead who wander until they reach their final destination in heaven or hell. As for demons, they are ruled over by Satan, who also appears in the Bible. He was said to be a fallen angel, and he is also known as Samael, Lucifer, or simply the Devil.

Each of these supernatural creatures has a purpose. Angels make their home in heaven and serve God in any way they are asked—for example, delivering messages in dreams, or serving as invisible guardians. One angel guards us until we are born, while another comes for us at the end of our lives.

Just as angels represent the forces of good and are helpful to people, demons represent the forces of evil and pose a great danger. In the Jewish view, they make their home in the Kingdom of Demons, but their primary role is to try to lead people astray. Thus a bride who is not careful may end up marrying a demon instead of her intended groom, while a man may find himself wed to his bride's demonic double.

After people die, their souls are said to take leave of their bodies as spirits. Sometimes a spirit haunts a house or another place as a ghost or visits the living while they are dreaming or even while they are awake. But the true goal of a righteous spirit is to travel to heaven, while an evil spirit must spend a year in Jewish hell, called *Gehenna*.

Belief in such things as demon marriages and the existence of ghosts gave birth to many remarkable tales. This book is a collection of nine of the best supernatural tales of this kind. They come from a wide range of countries, from Eastern Europe to the Middle East. Some stories are as much as 1500 years old, while others were recently collected in Israel and are still being told to this day.

In these tales, anything is possible: A newborn child can sit up in bed and tell a long story; a clever rabbi can steal a sword from the Angel of Death; a bride on her way to be married can be trapped in a stone; and a boy can be saved by the princess of demons. These stories gave order to all of existence for those who heard them. They explained the roles of these supernatural creatures and, to this day, serve as miracle stories as well as warning tales.

Do angels, spirits, and demons really exist? Do they whisper among themselves far too quietly for us to hear? Whether we believe in them or not is for each of us to decide. These tales let us glimpse a world in which good and evil creatures beckon to us everywhere, and rooms are filled with angels and ghosts.

I

The Kingdom of Angels

Angels serve

as messengers

of God.

1. The Angel's Gift

Long ago there was a wise rabbi who loved his wife dearly. They lived together like a pair of doves. But there was one thing missing from their lives: They were without children.

When a woman in their town could not have a child, she would ask the rabbi for help. He would give her an amulet, a piece of parchment on which he had written the name of an angel, which she would put in a case and wear around her neck. Everyone said that these amulets were remarkably effective, and so they were.

Now, the name that he wrote on each parchment was Lailah—for she was the angel in charge of guarding children until they were born.

For many years, the rabbi's wife watched as her husband gave out amulets that made it possible for other women to bear children, while she herself remained childless. At last, she could not resist asking, "Why can't you write an amulet for us as you do for all the others?"

"The others need the amulet to strengthen their faith," the rabbi replied. "But our faith in God is already strong. Surely God will send us the blessing of a child. Let us be patient."

That very night, the rabbi and his wife each had a vivid dream in which the angel Lailah appeared to them as a beautiful woman. She revealed that God had granted their wish. Within a year they would become the parents of a child with a very special soul—and they were told to name that child Samuel.

When they awoke, the rabbi and his wife were amazed to discover that they had dreamed the same dream. Lailah had appeared to both of them and had told them what they longed to hear—that they would be blessed with a child of their own.

Before the year was out, the rabbi's wife did give birth to a baby boy, whom they named Samuel, as the angel had requested. The midwife who delivered the child was the first to notice that he was born with his face aglow. In fact, the light from Samuel's face lit up the room.

And when the rabbi placed his newborn son in the cradle, he saw that the baby did not have the usual indentation above his lips that is seen on every other face.

The rabbi turned to his wife. "Surely the light that surrounds him is a sign that God has given us a great blessing, just as the angel Lailah promised."

No sooner were those words spoken than a voice replied, "Do you know my friend Lailah?" The surprised parents looked around the room to see who was there, but the only person they saw was the baby.

"Who just spoke?" the rabbi asked.

"Your son," the voice said.

The rabbi's wife sat up in bed. "But you are only an infant."

"Yes, Mother," the baby continued, "but the angel Lailah has given me a great gift. She touches all the other babies on earth above the lips just before they are born, making them forget all that they know. That is what makes the indentation above their lips. But Lailah let me retain all the memories of the world I left behind."

The rabbi was amazed. "What world is that?" he asked.

Samuel's face glowed even more brightly. "The world of Paradise," he said. "Have everyone from the synagogue gather here, and I will tell my story."

The rabbi ran to the synagogue and asked everyone to follow him home. Neighbors came out of their houses to see why the rabbi was rushing by. "Come see for yourselves," he cried.

Soon the small home of the rabbi and his wife was filled with people, all crowded close to the cradle. And the infant sat up, much to their amazement, and began to speak.

"As you know, my name is Samuel. I came here with the help of the angel Lailah. It is Lailah who brought my soul and body together, and Lailah who guarded me for all the months before I was born. In the womb, she lit a lamp and read to me from the Book of Mysteries while I slept.

"Now, Lailah is required to press her finger against the lip of all newborn children, so they will forget everything that happened before they were born. But Lailah wanted me to remember."

"Why?" asked the rabbi, who could hardly believe that his infant son was speaking.

"Because I was a storyteller named Samuel in my previous life. Let me explain. I always traveled from city to city, telling of the miracles of the rabbis. After many years, I announced I was going to tell my last tale.

"People came from all over, certain it would be the best tale I had ever told. From the very beginning of the tale, all who listened fell into a trance. Nothing existed for them except the words I wove. The story seemed endless, and that was how they wanted it to be.

"But then I fell ill and died before I could finish the tale. Not only was there an uproar on earth, but there was one in heaven as well, for the angels were also waiting for the story's end.

"Now, when I reached heaven, the angels crowded around me, anxious for me to finish the tale. But I refused.

"'Why?' they cried, for their curiosity is far more intense than that of any human.

"'Because,' I replied, 'I must first complete it on earth.'

"'But that is impossible,' said the angels, 'for you are now among us, and you can't go back.'

"'But I must,' I said, and after that I was completely mute. One century, two, three centuries in all. The angels saw that I would not relent. And after three hundred years, they were so anxious to hear the rest of my story that they begged God to send my soul back to earth so that I could finish telling the tale. God agreed and asked the angel Lailah to serve as my guide. That is why Lailah has permitted me to remember all that I knew."

Everyone moved even closer to the cradle and begged Samuel to tell them the story that had remained unfinished for so long. When Samuel agreed to do so, a great wind blew through the house. And when everyone looked up, they were amazed to see a multitude of angels crowded beneath the roof, all waiting for the story to be told. Then the people understood that everything they had heard that day must be true.

So Samuel began to retell the tale that he had begun in another lifetime. It was a long tale, still unfinished at midnight, still unfinished when the sun rose. But no one even thought of leaving. They were

spellbound. And when the tale finally came to an end, everyone awoke as if from a dream.

Samuel felt a great sense of relief when he finished. Then the angel Lailah stepped forward, looking exactly as she had in the dreams of the rabbi and his wife. She kissed Samuel and told him it was the most beautiful story she had ever heard. She sang him to sleep with a haunting lullaby and tapped her finger once above his lips, making an indentation.

Then everyone watched in awe as Lailah and the other angels departed. The wind from their wings awakened the infant Samuel, who had now forgotten everything except that he was hungry. He began to cry out for his mother to feed him. And everyone understood that Samuel had become an infant like any other, now that his story had been told.

POLAND: ORAL TRADITION

2. The Angel's Sword

It was as well known in heaven as it was on earth that Rabbi Joshua ben Levi was a perfect saint. So when the time came for the Angel of Death to collect his soul and bring it to heaven, God said to the angel: "Take care to respect Rabbi Joshua and try to be gentle with him." This the angel promised to do.

Before long, the Angel of Death was knocking at the door of Rabbi Joshua's house. At that time, Rabbi Joshua was studying the Torah, and he did not like to be interrupted.

Now, many brave men and women have found themselves quaking with fear at the sight of the Angel of Death. But Rabbi Joshua was not the least bit frightened. "What is it?" he asked. "Why have you interrupted my studies?"

The angel said, "Rabbi, do you not recognize me?"

"Of course I know who you are," said Rabbi Joshua. "You are the Angel of Death."

"That is true," said the angel. "And if you know who I am, then you must know why I have come here."

"I know who you are," said Rabbi Joshua. "But I can't read your mind."

"Rabbi," said the angel, trying to be as polite as possible, "God has sent me on a mission to take your soul."

"Go away!" said Rabbi Joshua. "I'm not going anywhere." And he slammed the door, determined to complete his work on earth.

The Angel of Death didn't know what to do, so he returned to heaven to consult with God. "Master of the Universe, Rabbi Joshua refuses to come with me," said the angel.

God said: "Go back to Rabbi Joshua and try again. If he refuses to come with you, ask him if he would like you to show him his place in the Garden of Eden."

So the Angel of Death returned to Rabbi Joshua's house and knocked at his door. But Rabbi Joshua recognized his knock and refused to open the door, "Go away! I would never entrust my soul to you." For he did not have much regard for that angel without mercy who struck terror in the hearts of all.

"In that case," said the Angel of Death, "would you at least like to see your place in the Garden of Eden?"

Now, all his life Rabbi Joshua had wondered about the place where he would spent eternity, so he agreed to accompany the angel to the Garden of Eden. But when Rabbi Joshua opened the door, he saw that the Angel of Death was carrying his sword. "I'm sorry," said the rabbi, "but I will not go with you as long as you're carrying that terrible weapon. If you want me to come with you, give it to me."

The Angel of Death was taken aback by this demand. As long as he could remember, he had never been without his sword, and he did not want to give it up. But God had told him to respect the wishes of Rabbi Joshua, so the angel reluctantly agreed. Then he lifted the rabbi onto his wings and carried him toward the Garden of Eden.

When they were almost there, Rabbi Joshua said, "Fly higher. I want to see the whole Garden." So the angel did, and Rabbi Joshua was able to glimpse that unforgettable Garden, which has no equal in the world.

"I never imagined that it would be this beautiful," said Rabbi Joshua. "But now I would like to see the place in the Garden where I will spend eternity."

So the angel, still carrying Rabbi Joshua on his wings, flew over a meadow by one of the four rivers that run through Eden and showed the rabbi his resting place.

"Now," said Rabbi Joshua, "I want to sit on the wall of the Garden."

So the angel took him there.

Rabbi Joshua knew that the Angel of Death is not allowed to enter Eden. So a moment after they sat down on the wall, Rabbi Joshua leaped into the Garden, still carrying the angel's sword.

"Come out of there," the angel cried, "and give back my sword!" But Rabbi Joshua refused. "I will never come out. And I will never give back your sword!"

The Angel of Death did not know what to do, so he returned to heaven and consulted with God.

"Master of the Universe, Rabbi Joshua has escaped me and has vowed never to come out of Eden. Even worse, he refuses to give back my sword."

God said to the angel: "See if Rabbi Joshua has ever broken a vow. If he has, then this vow can also be broken. But if not, this vow can't be broken either."

So the Angel of Death checked and found that Rabbi Joshua had never broken a vow. Meanwhile, several days had passed and something strange had taken place in the world. No one had died, for the Angel of Death was unable to take the souls of the living without his sword.

In great frustration, the Angel of Death returned to the wall of the Garden of Eden and called out to Rabbi Joshua, "If you won't come out, at least give me back my sword."

"No," said Rabbi Joshua. "Why should I do that? Go away and leave me alone."

But then a voice came forth from heaven, saying: "Give him back his sword, my son. He needs it to perform his duties."

Now, when Rabbi Joshua heard God's voice, he realized that he could no longer hold on to the angel's sword. But he had one more idea. He told the angel, "I will give back your sword. But only if you vow not to show it when you come to take anyone's soul." And the angel wanted his sword so badly that he made the vow.

That is how Rabbi Joshua ben Levi managed to enter the Garden of Eden, where the souls of the righteous make their home, while he was still alive. And that is why the Angel of Death no longer uses his sword to frighten people when he comes to take their souls, for he, too, cannot break a vow.

BABYLON: FIFTH CENTURY

3. The Angel's Daughter

Once upon a time there was a lad named Yoel who was the youngest of seven sons. One night Yoel had a haunting dream in which he was in a strange city in a strange land. Crowds lined the streets, and standing beside him was an old man with a feather in his cap.

"What is everyone waiting for?" asked Yoel.

"Our princess," said the old man. "She is the daughter of an angel and lives in a palace of pearls on a golden mountain. Once a year she rides through the city streets with her golden dove. When we see that she still has the dove, we know our city will be blessed with good fortune for yet another year."

The crowd began to cheer, and Yoel watched a young lady of astonishing beauty, dressed in a white gown, come riding down the street on a white horse. Perched on her shoulder was a golden dove, whose feathers reflected the sun. She was the most beautiful girl Yoel had ever seen, and he lost his heart to her.

Suddenly thunder roared and lightning flashed, although no storm clouds darkened the sky. The white horse reared up, pawing the air with its hooves, and the golden dove took flight.

The princess cried out, and everyone raced after the dove, but it flew high over their heads, then disappeared from sight.

Yoel wanted more than anything to catch that dove, so he could take it back to the beautiful princess. He searched for it everywhere and finally found himself alone near a tree covered with white flowers. And there, on the very top branch, was the golden dove.

He climbed up the tree and was within an arm's reach of the bird when another clap of thunder awakened him from his dream.

Yoel opened his eyes and saw that rain was pouring down as in the days of Noah and the Flood. Thunder and lightning split the sky, but Yoel could think of nothing but his dream and how sad he was that it had ended before he could capture the golden dove and return it to the princess who was the daughter of an angel.

That very day, Yoel's widowed mother said to him: "Your six older brothers have each married beautiful brides, and now it is time for you to be wed."

But Yoel was still remembering his dream. "The only one I will marry is the daughter of an angel," he said, "the one I saw in my dream."

Yoel's mother and his brothers and his friends all tried to get him to change his mind, but Yoel vowed never to marry any other. And every day and night Yoel prayed that he might be blessed to marry the beautiful girl of his dreams.

A few weeks later, Yoel again dreamed of the old man with the feather in his cap. This time they met in a forest, and the old man said: "The princess cannot bear to live any longer without the golden dove, so her mother, the Queen, has announced that the princess will wed whoever finds the dove and brings it back to her."

"But where can I find it?" Yoel asked.

"The dove has been captured by Azazel, a fallen angel, who is chained upside down in a canyon of sharp stones, deep in the desert Dudael, beyond the Mountains of Darkness," said the old man. "But beware—even though Azazel is a prisoner, he has not lost his evil powers."

Then the old man handed Yoel the golden feather from his cap, and just as Yoel closed his fingers around it, he woke up, still holding that golden feather in his hand. It seemed impossible, but there it was, glowing as brightly as a mirror. Yoel knew it was a sign that he might still accomplish his quest. And when Yoel peered into that strange mirror, he saw something that took his breath away: the golden dove of his dream, sitting in a golden cage, in a very dark place. Yoel knew he must somehow find the dove for the princess—and the enchanted feather gave him hope.

That very day, Yoel set out for the Mountains of Darkness. He traveled for many months, through cities and towns, fields and forests, until at last those dark mountains were towering above him. But he had no idea how to cross them to get to the other side.

Now, in the little village at the foot of those mountains, there was an inn where Yoel stopped to have some dinner. While he sat eating, he overheard two merchants talking at the next table.

One said, "It's too bad there is no easy way to cross the Mountains of Darkness."

"Yes, there is," said the other, "but I can't can't tell you about it."

"Why not?" asked the first merchant.

"Because," said the second, "I have dreamed three times that I must reveal the secret only to someone with a golden feather."

When Yoel heard this, he knew that luck was still with him. As soon as the first merchant left, Yoel showed the feather to the second.

"You must be the one I've been waiting for," said the merchant, staring wide-eyed at the glowing feather. He led Yoel behind the inn to a steep path that twisted and turned on its way up the mountain. Then he plunged into the underbrush, scrambling over rocks and branches with Yoel at his heels. Finally they reached an old tree growing there. The merchant said, "Look behind the tree. You will find the entrance to a cave there." Yoel pushed branches aside and saw a narrow opening. "Go through that cave," the merchant continued, "and when you come out the other end, you will have crossed the Mountains of Darkness."

"Will I have reached the desert Dudael?" asked Yoel.

"No," said the merchant, "but you'll see a path that will take you there."

Yoel was delighted that he had found a way to cross those legendary mountains. He thanked the merchant and entered the dark cave. He was feeling along the sides of the cave with his hands and stumbling over stones when he suddenly remembered the feather in his pocket. He pulled it out and found that the glowing feather lit up the cave like a torch. For three days and three nights, Yoel traveled through that cave, with the enchanted feather lighting the way.

When Yoel finally reached the end of the cave, he saw a great forest that stretched in all directions, as far as he could see and far beyond. At first Yoel was afraid of becoming lost there, but then he saw a path running through the forest, just as the merchant had said.

For six days, Yoel followed the winding path through the forest, seeing no one, for few traveled there. But on the seventh day, a carriage appeared behind him, pulled by two white horses. Yoel couldn't imagine why such a fine carriage was in that lonely forest, but as it drew near, he saw that the driver was the old man from his dream, the man who had given him the golden feather. Inside the carriage was a veiled woman dressed in black.

"Climb up beside me," the driver said. "It is a long road you have taken."

"If your mistress permits," said Yoel. And when the woman nodded her head, he climbed up beside the driver. He wanted to ask the old man many questions about his quest, but the old man had started singing, and Yoel didn't want to interrupt his song.

Before long, Yoel noticed that the wheels of the carriage never seemed to touch the ground, so fast did the horses fly through that forest. And by nightfall, the vast desert Dudael stretched out before them. How had they traveled such a great distance in one short day? There the carriage stopped, and the driver said, "It's been a pleasure to share your company, but now we must turn back. From here on, you must travel on your own."

The astonished lad got down from the carriage, thanked the old man and the veiled woman, and watched the carriage disappear back into the forest.

Yoel looked around and saw an old olive tree on the border between the forest and the desert. It was bent over like an old man but was still bearing fruit. He picked a handful of olives and ate to his heart's content. Then he lay down and slept.

While Yoel was sleeping, the carriage silently returned. The veiled woman in black got out and knelt beside him. She whispered in his ear: "Yoel, know that a tribe living nearby is about to send a goat to Azazel, as it does every year. That goat is known as the scapegoat, because it carries their sins. Follow that goat, and it will lead you to him. But do not let anyone in the tribe see you. So too must you keep yourself hidden from Azazel, lest he send the demons of the desert to harm you." Even though Yoel was asleep, he heard every phrase that was spoken. The words were as clear to him as if they had been inscribed on stone.

When Yoel awoke that morning, he saw smoke rising in the distance and walked toward it. Soon he saw people chanting and singing around an altar, so he hid behind a rock and watched. Suddenly everyone shouted, "Go to Azazel!" and chased a goat into the desert. That is when Yoel realized that this must be the very tribe he was seeking, and the very goat he was supposed to follow.

From his hiding place, Yoel watched where the goat went, and as soon as the people left, he followed it. It ran across the desert and into a canyon, and there it descended into the depths. Yoel shuddered as darkness fell. He realized he had entered the evil realm of Azazel.

Soon it was pitch-black, but Yoel dared not take out the gleaming feather to light his way. What if one of Azazel's demons saw him? He could no longer see the goat or hear its hooves striking the stones, but he continued climbing down.

Suddenly he heard a voice say, "Be careful! You are about to fall into a pit."

Yoel froze in his tracks. "Who are you?" he cried.

"Take out the feather and see for yourself." With trembling hands, Yoel took out the golden feather. He saw that he was standing on the very edge of an abyss, and the voice he heard was coming from—the goat!

"Can you really speak?" Yoel asked.

"Don't question miracles," the goat said. "I was sent here to help you—but don't ask who sent me."

Yoel sighed. "Wherever you came from, I am grateful you saved me from falling. But what must we do to save the golden dove?"

"Azazel keeps the golden dove in a cage by his side," said the goat. "God chained him upside down in punishment for his evil deeds, but his power is very great, and many evil demons serve him. Yet I may be able to help you. Even now Azazel and his demons are awaiting my arrival. They long to wrap themselves in the sins I am bearing. If I can distract them, you may be able to snatch away the golden dove and climb out of this pit of evil." Yoel agreed to try, and he followed the goat into the very heart of darkness.

When they neared the cave of Azazel, Yoel put the feather in his pocket and hid behind a boulder while the goat bleated loudly. As it had expected, hordes of demons and fiery serpents came swarming out of the cave, hissing and shouting, chasing after the goat, for they knew that Azazel would richly reward whoever caught it for him. The goat dashed away, leading them far from the cave and giving Yoel a chance to creep inside.

The presence of evil in that dark cave hung like a sword. It frightened Yoel, but he felt the feather in his pocket and found the strength to go on.

Slowly, Yoel's eyes adjusted to the darkness, and he made his way over rocks, across underground streams, and down long passages. Just as he was wondering if the cave would ever end, he saw a terrifying sight— the dim outline of the fallen angel, chained upside down against the cave wall. Close by, something golden was shimmering in the darkness—the golden dove inside its cage! A shiver went down Yoel's spine. The dove was very close, but so was the fallen angel.

Yoel took a deep breath—and Azazel heard him. "Who's there?" the fallen angel roared. "Why aren't you out chasing the goat?" Yoel was so startled that he almost fainted, but he knew he had to reply or Azazel would know he was an intruder.

·"The goat has been captured," Yoel said, "and they are bringing it back now."

This seemed to satisfy the fallen angel, for he blissfully closed his eyes and began to chant: "Bring on the goat, the garlic, and the wine—the goat, the garlic, and the wine—the goat . . ." While Azazel was howling his song, Yoel ran forward and snatched the cage with the golden dove and raced up long passages, across underground streams, and over rocks until he reached the entrance to the cave.

He was climbing upward, out of the deep canyon, when he heard Azazel begin to scream: "The golden bird is gone!" Yoel knew that the fallen angel would send forth his demons to find the bird—so he climbed even faster. And that's when the goat reappeared. "Follow me," it said, for it knew the shortest route away from that pit of hell. They heard screaming demons swarming after them, but as they climbed higher, the screams grew fainter. The sense of evil that Yoel had felt so strongly began to disappear. And when they finally reached the top of the canyon, they were free from the evil powers of Azazel.

As they stood under the stars, Yoel thanked the goat for helping him save the golden bird. "But how did you manage to distract them for so long?" he asked.

The goat replied, "I used my magic, of course. Every time they cornered me, I disappeared and reappeared somewhere else. Now we are beyond their evil power."

"But where is the palace of pearls, where the princess lives?" Yoel asked.

"I will take you there," the goat replied.

So Yoel climbed onto the back of the goat and grasped one of its horns, holding the cage of the golden bird in his other hand. He found himself soaring through the heavens on the enchanted goat. They were flying high above earth. Soon they saw something shining in the distance. It was the palace of pearls on the golden mountain.

Suddenly, Yoel found himself standing before the door of that palace, the cage of the golden dove still in his hands. The goat was nowhere to be seen. He was sorry he had not had a chance to bid it farewell, but he was eager to see the princess, so he knocked on the great door. It opened at once, and there was the old man who had given him the feather in the first place. Yoel smiled and handed it back to the old man, who stuck it into his cap.

"Welcome, Yoel," he said. "We have been awaiting you—and the dove." Then he led Yoel down a long hallway and through intricate double doors made entirely of pearls. Yoel found himself in a palace chamber in which everything was made of pearls. There, seated on a throne of pearls, was the Queen, and standing beside her was the veiled woman, dressed in black. Yoel's curiosity was even greater than before. He handed the cage to the Queen. She opened it—and the dove immediately flew to the veiled woman, perched on her hand, and began to sing. The woman removed her veil, and Yoel saw that she was the beautiful princess. She cast off the black garment, and beneath it was the white dress she had been wearing when Yoel first saw her in his dream. The radiance of her smile was as brilliant as that of the gleaming bird.

The Queen said: "Yoel, you have done a great deed. The princess was so sad to lose the dove and its beautiful song that I promised that whoever found it could marry her. Many princes tried, but all came back empty-handed. Only you have succeeded in this quest."

Just then Yoel heard the beating of wings. When he looked up, he saw a glowing being standing in that room, and he realized he was in the presence of an angel. The angel said: "Welcome, Yoel, and come in peace."

Now that voice was very familiar, and Yoel cried out, "I know that voice. It's the voice of the goat!"

"Yes," said the angel, "I was the goat who guided you. But you were very brave to enter the lair of Azazel and snatch the golden dove from his side."

Then the angel, who was none other than the angel Gabriel, said: "Yoel, even before you were born, it was destined that you would marry my daughter, the princess. But everyone must fulfill his own destiny, and in finding the golden dove, you have fulfilled yours. Now let the wedding take place."

So it was that a great wedding was held, and Yoel married the princess, the daughter of an angel, and together they ruled that kingdom from a palace of pearls on a golden mountain, and they lived happily ever after.

BUKHARA: ORAL TRADITION

II
The Kingdom of Spirits

Spirits of the dead

haunt this world

as ghosts.

4. A Roomful of Ghosts

An air of mystery surrounded Rabbi Mordecai of Chernobyl. Everyone spoke in awe of his powers. It was said that he had a magic staff, like that of Moses, and that he knew how to repair the souls of the living as well as those of the dead. Now, Rabbi Mordecai was coming to spend the night as a guest at Jacob's home, and Jacob was very curious to meet him. But most of all he wanted to solve one of the great mysteries about the rabbi: what he did at night.

It was Rabbi Mordecai's custom to remain alone in his room for several hours every evening. That in itself was not so unusual, but there had been reports of strange voices coming from his room when he was alone in there. And now, since the rabbi was staying at Jacob's house, the boy decided to hide in the rabbi's room, so that he could see for himself.

That night, Jacob climbed into a wooden wardrobe in the rabbi's room and pulled the doors closed, leaving them open just a crack. It was dark and eerie inside the wardrobe, but Jacob's curiosity was greater than his fear. So he stayed, barely breathing, waiting for the rabbi to arrive. At last the rabbi came into the room and closed the door. From his hiding place, Jacob peered out and saw that the rabbi was smoking a pipe. The smoke of the pipe swirled around the room, creating clouds of smoke. Then, all at once, Jacob began to hear voices speaking from those clouds. Not one or two, but a multitude of voices, all of them pleading for the rabbi's attention. But where were all these people? Jacob could see that only the rabbi was in the room, yet he still heard voices all around. That is when Jacob understood that they must be some kinds of ghosts, who had sought out the rabbi.

Being surrounded by a roomful of invisible ghosts frightened Jacob, and he wished he had never thought of hiding in that wardrobe. But now it was too late. So he listened to the stories of the ghosts who begged the rabbi to save them, so that they could ascend to Paradise.

These were souls who had become lost on their way to Paradise and had been wandering for hundreds of years, searching for the gate of heaven so they could ascend on high. Rabbi Mordecai showed them the invisible gate, and the lost souls threaded their way into heaven.

Now Jacob saw through the crack between the cabinet doors that Rabbi Mordecai had picked up a pen and had begun to write. Jacob guessed he must be writing some kind of blessings or holy names for the invisible spirits who approached him. For as soon as he would finish writing one, a spirit would snatch up the slip of paper and carry it off.

Next Jacob heard the sad voice of a woman who was telling the rabbi her story. She too had been condemned to be a wandering spirit, but after many years, she was seeking out the rabbi to repair her soul and guide her into heaven. But this time the rabbi told her that he could not help her. He said, "There is only one who can help you. That is the spirit of a rich man who is buried in a cemetery. That rich man never gave a single ruble to charity in his life. Now, you must go to him and beg for a ruble. And if he gives it to you, you will be saving his soul, and because you have saved a soul, your own soul, too, will be saved."

"Rabbi," said the woman, "there is nothing I want more than to obey you, but how will I find this rich man when I don't know what his name was or where he is buried?"

"Don't worry," said Rabbi Mordecai. "Surely Jacob, who is hiding in the wardrobe, will show you the way!"

No sooner had Jacob heard these words than he gasped with fear. How did the rabbi know he was hiding there? And what did he mean by saying that Jacob would show her the way? All at once, the doors of the wardrobe swung open, and Rabbi Mordecai stood before him. Jacob wanted to dash out of the room, but he was paralyzed with fear. At last he found the strength to speak, and he begged the rabbi not to make him go to a cemetery at night.

"Be brave!" said the rabbi, so firmly that Jacob suddenly felt far braver than he had a moment before. "I will give you my staff," said the rabbi. "As long as you hold it tightly, there is nothing to worry about."

Then the rabbi picked up his staff and handed it to Jacob. And the instant his fingers took hold of that staff, Jacob saw for the first time the great crowd of ghosts that had flocked together in the rabbi's room. At that instant, he suddenly felt himself lifted, as if by an invisible hand, and flung out the window, where he continued to fly through the air, clinging to the rabbi's staff. He seemed to be flying as high as the moon, and he saw the stars close by on every side. Then Jacob saw that the ghost of the woman was following close behind him, as that invisible hand propelled him through the heavens.

All of a sudden, Jacob found himself descending, and soon he was

standing in the center of a cemetery. What he saw there astonished him, for the ghosts of the dead were sitting beside their tombstones or flying around. And because he was holding the rabbi's staff, Jacob understood what they said to each other. But Jacob had no time to listen to their conversations, for he found himself standing before a large tomb, which he knew must be that of the rich man. And seated beside it was the rich man's ghost, who was listening to the ghost of the woman begging for his help. All that she asked for was a single ruble. And Jacob wondered if the rich man would still be a miser even after his death.

But Jacob was very surprised to see the ghost of the rich man begin to weep as he gave a ruble to the ghost of the woman. "Ever since I died," he said, "I have sought to make up for my miserly ways. But until now, every single ghost has refused my charity, saying that what was held back while a person was alive cannot be given after he has died. You are the first who was willing to receive anything from me." The woman also wept, for she realized how much good she had done. And now a path appeared out of the darkness, a rainbow of light, for the two spirits to follow into heaven.

As for Jacob, he watched them disappear up that path, and he was happy for them both. Only then he remembered that he was standing in a cemetery late at night, surrounded by ghosts. Jacob pulled the rabbi's staff closer and wished to himself that he were back home. And no sooner had this thought crossed his mind than he found himself standing before the open wardrobe in the rabbi's room. And the rabbi said, "You did very well, Jacob, but what took you so long?"

EASTERN EUROPE: NINETEENTH CENTURY

5. King David Is Alive

There once were two students in a Jewish academy in Poland who dreamed about Jerusalem day and night. They were determined to set foot in the Holy Land. And of all the holy places in Jerusalem, they were especially eager to visit the tomb of King David, for he was their hero. They loved to read his psalms and could recite every one by heart.

At last, they set forth on their journey, even though they didn't have a single zloty. They traveled for months, but God's grace accompanied them every step of the way. In all the towns they passed through, they were offered hospitality by Jews who wanted to help them on their sacred journey.

When they reached Constantinople, they stowed away on a ship headed for the Holy Land. But their small store of food and water soon ran out. They were growing weak. Then they happened to see a Jewish sailor saying the morning prayers in the hold, so they slipped out of hiding to pray with him. And when they told him about their hunger and thirst, he promised to secretly bring them food and water. Thus they could stay hidden for the remainder of the voyage.

When they finally reached the Holy Land, they set out for Jerusalem. It seemed so beautiful to them that they thought they had entered Paradise. They thanked God for bringing them to the Holy City. But they did not know how to find King David's tomb. While they were wondering where it was, an old man suddenly appeared before them. He was wearing a goatskin mantle and was walking with a staff. They asked him the way to Mount Zion, and he led them there himself.

At the foot of the mountain, he told them they had reached King David's tomb. "This is where King David sleeps," he said. "Most of the world thinks that sleep is eternal, but really he is waiting to be awakened, so that he can arise and bestow his blessings on the world."

The two students were thrilled. How often they had dreamed of meeting King David, and now it seemed that such a miracle might be possible.

"Tell us," said one of the students, "how can he be awakened?"

"Listen carefully," the old man said. "You must ascend Mount Zion until you reach the entrance of King David's tomb. Once you are inside, go down the stone steps until you reach the bottom. There you will find an iron door that is locked. If you can find a way to open that door, you will find King David sleeping in the cavern on the other side.

"But beware! Once you enter that cavern, you will be blinded by visions of gold, silver, and diamonds. These are only illusions, set to tempt you from your purpose. Ignore them and find the jug of water near the head of King David.

"That jug contains water from the Garden of Eden. Pour that water over King David's hands three times as he stretches them toward you, for King David will arise when we are worthy of it. By your virtue and merit, he will arise and redeem us. Amen, and may this come to pass."

The students realized that the old man must be Elijah, for who else would know such heavenly secrets? And no sooner had he finished speaking than the old man disappeared. The students understood that they had been given a sacred duty, but the old man had not explained how to get past that iron door. Still, they ascended Mount Zion, exactly as Elijah had told them to do, and they went down into the depths of King David's tomb.

Everything was just as Elijah had said it would be. They descended the stone stairs and reached the iron door. But they could not open it, no matter how hard they tried. And there was no key in sight. What were they supposed to do?

"Let us turn to King David for inspiration," said one of the young men. They started reciting all of King David's psalms. And the moment they finished saying the last one, they heard hinges creaking. The psalms were the key! They had discovered the very secret that opened the door, and they rushed inside.

As soon as they entered the cavern, they saw King David lying on a couch with a jug of water at his head. At the same time, they saw gleaming treasures of every kind filling the tomb. At that moment, King David reached out toward them. But the young men were so dazzled by the gold and jewels that they forgot to pour water on the king's outstretched hands. In his anguish, his hands fell back, and immediately the king's image disappeared. So too did all the jewels vanish, for they had been only an illusion.

The young men stood heartbroken in the dim cavern. They realized they had let the opportunity to bring King David to life slip through their fingers, and now it was too late.

POLAND: ORAL TRADITION

6. The Lost Melody

Rabbi Abraham was a wandering musician. He went from village to village playing his violin at the weddings of the poor. His music made others happy, and he asked for nothing more than a meal and a place to sleep.

Now Rabbi Abraham especially loved playing at orphans' weddings and at the end of every Sabbath. His favorite songs were Hasidic *niguns*, haunting melodies without words. During the summer, when the windows were wide open, the sound of his violin was heard up and down the street. Old people as well as young listened to his wonderful playing, which brought joy to a neighborhood that was sad and poor.

On holidays, too, Rabbi Abraham could be heard playing his violin, which had been in his family for many generations. He played on the eve of Hanukah after lighting the candles. And he played on the eve of Purim.

Each year it was his custom, right after the Purim meal in his house, to take his violin and go to entertain sick and poor people. When he played for poor families, the children would hum along and the women would clap. And before he left, Rabbi Abraham would taste some wine and continue on his way to the next house.

Now one year, the holiday of Purim took place during an exception-ally cold winter. Deep snow covered the ground, and a strong wind shook roofs and shutters.

Rabbi Abraham was more than sixty years old, and his wife, Bilabasha, asked him not to go out that year. But he was determined to lighten the hearts of the sick and poor on Purim, as he had done since his youth.

So Rabbi Abraham left home and went from house to house playing for the people. Nor did he refuse any food or drink that the poor gave him in thanks.

When Rabbi Abraham had not come home by midnight, Bilabasha began to worry. By one o'clock, she started to worry even more. And when the old clock showed two, Rabbi Abraham's wife woke Rabbi Levi, the driver, from a deep sleep.

Rabbi Levi hitched a horse to the sleigh and went with Bilabasha to the house of the village rabbi. They woke the rabbi, and with the rabbi's assistant, the shamash, they lit several lamps and went to search for Rabbi Abraham. Every place they went, they were told yes, he had been there. He had played his violin, drunk a glass of wine, and gone on his way.

At last they returned home without having found Rabbi Abraham. The shamash was weary, but he did not return to bed, for it was time to open the ancient synagogue. But what did he see when he went inside? There was Rabbi Abraham, sitting up in the hallway of the synagogue, his ancient violin in his hand. He was playing a beautiful melody, which the shamash had never heard before.

"Rabbi Abraham!" cried the shamash. "Are you all right? Where have you been?"

"Don't bother me," said Rabbi Abraham. "I must not forget the melody that I just learned from Rabbi Menashe, the cantor."

"But Rabbi Menashe died many years ago," the shamash said.

"I know," said Rabbi Abraham. And he played the song over and over until he knew it by heart. Then he turned to the shamash. "Let me tell you what happened:

"I went from house to house, playing my violin, as I do every Purim. Everyone was very generous, and perhaps I drank a little too much wine.

"On my way home, I decided to take a shortcut through the yard of the synagogue—even though I have heard that the dead pray in the synagogue every night. While passing in front of the gate, I heard a voice from inside the synagogue say, 'Will Rabbi Abraham, the son of Jacob the Cohen, come forth and pray?' At that instant I was filled with terror. Who was calling me? I wanted to escape, but I knew that I had no choice but to go inside. For when you are called to pray before the Torah, you must do it.

"As I approached the door of the synagogue, my legs were trembling. All at once, the door opened as if by itself, and I peered inside. There I saw that the Torah had been taken out of the Ark and lay open. And standing before it I saw ghostly figures as transparent as spiderwebs.

"Shivering with fear, I took my place before the Torah, made the blessing, and was ready to run away. But all at once I saw Rabbi Menashe, the cantor, hurrying toward me. I was very surprised to see him, for I knew that he was no longer among the living.

"'Rabbi Abraham,' he said, 'please, have mercy. There is something that I must tell you.'

"I tried to remain calm, although I could hear my heart beating. I nodded for him to go on.

"The ghostly figure said, 'There is a melody I composed just before I died, which I took with me to the grave. But it is a great burden for me, for the song has never been heard by anyone else. Let me share it with you, so that you can play it for others. And as soon as you do, my melody will be set free, and you, Rabbi Abraham, will be rewarded with a long life.'

"When I heard this, I realized that I had not come there by chance. And even though I was speaking to a spirit, my fear vanished, and I listened carefully as Rabbi Menashe began to sing that *niggun*. And as soon as he finished, he and all the other ghostly figures vanished, and I took out my violin and played, so as not to forget it. Now I must play it again and again, till my fingers know it by heart." And so he did, while the shamash listened in amazement.

The next day, Rabbi Abraham sang that magnificent melody for the first time in front of the congregation of the old synagogue. And all who were present agreed that it was truly a haunting melody, the likes of which had never been heard.

GERMANY: ORAL TRADITION

III

The Kingdom of Demons

Demons

are forces of evil

who try to lead a person

astray.

7. Yona and the River Demon

There once was a poor girl named Yona who was engaged to be married. But for years the marriage had been delayed, because the groom's family expected to receive a precious gift—a dowry—from the bride's family. Yona's father was so poor that he could not afford to pay it. So Yona herself worked hard to save enough for the dowry, washing head coverings for the women of the village.

Now, Yona washed those kerchiefs day and night. One evening, when Yona went down to the Bosporus River, the moon was shining brightly above the waters, and the image of the moon that floated on the water seemed as real as the moon itself. Suddenly, a handsome young man appeared before her. Yona wondered who he was, but she was not afraid of him, for he seemed gentle and charming.

"Why are you working so late at night?" he asked.

"I am earning money for my dowry," Yona replied.

The young man smiled. "I would like to contribute to it," he said. And he took two gold coins out of his pocket and gave them to her. Yona was very surprised by this gift. But before she could say anything, the young man turned away and disappeared into the night.

Yona put the two gold coins in the chest where she kept her dowry, and she decided to keep her meeting with the young man a secret.

The next evening, when she went back down to the river to wash kerchiefs, the young man appeared again. He was more handsome than ever. He asked Yona to lift her hand, and when she did, he put a golden bracelet on her arm, saying, "You are mine and I am yours." These words astonished Yona, but before she could say a word, the young man disappeared.

Nor did he come back after that night. Days and weeks passed, but Yona never saw him again. But each night, after she returned home from the river, she found that a new gold coin had appeared in the chest of her dowry, coins identical to the ones given to her by the young man on the night they had first met. With the help of the handsome young man, Yona succeeded in filling the chest. And the very night she completed the dowry, the handsome young man suddenly appeared at her door when Yona was alone in the house. He brought her a sack of flour and asked her to prepare a cake for him.

Yona did not know why he wanted her to do this, but she was grateful for all his gifts. So she went to work immediately, and soon the cake was ready. The young man asked her to share it with him. So Yona poured glasses of wine, and they ate cake and drank together. Then the young man said good-bye and took his leave.

The next day Yona and her family carried the chest to the home of her fiancé, as was the custom at that time. It was opened as part of an elaborate ceremony led by the village rabbi. But when they opened the chest, it was completely empty. Yona screamed and fainted.

When Yona finally recovered, the village rabbi, who had known her since she was born, tried to find out what had happened. At first Yona was reluctant to say anything about the young man, but at last she told them how she had met him at the river, and how his gifts had continued to accumulate in the chest. She also showed them the golden bracelet that he had given her on the second night, and told them about the cake she had baked for him, which they had shared together.

When the rabbi heard this story and saw the bracelet, he sighed. "Yona, that was no human you met—it was a river demon! For they approach anyone foolish enough to go down to the river at night, and they love, above all, to trick a young girl like yourself into marrying a demon. So when the demon put that bracelet on your wrist and spoke the words 'You are mine and I am yours,' that was a wedding vow. And when you shared that wine and cake with him, you were celebrating your own wedding, even though you did not know it."

Yona was horrified. Was it possible that she had been wed to a demon? She began to cry, and no one could console her. As for the family of the groom, they were not sure that a wedding with their son could still take place, because it seemed as if Yona had already been wed, even if she didn't know anything about it. Besides, the dowry chest was empty.

Everyone agreed that this was clearly a matter to be decided by a court of rabbis. So the village rabbi went down to the river that night and called upon the river demon who had married the maiden Yona. Much to his amazement, the handsome young man appeared out of nowhere. The rabbi said, "Why have you deceived poor Yona in this terrible way?"

The river demon answered, "All that matters is that she is mine."

"If that is what you believe," said the rabbi, "then you must come to a court of rabbis in three days. The court will decide if your marriage is valid and binding." And the demon agreed to appear before the court, for demons are bound by the laws of God as much as any man.

On the third day, the hearing was held by the court of rabbis. Yona's father testified that she had been engaged for many years to her fiancé, long before she had ever met the demon. And the father of the groom also testified that this was true.

Then it was Yona's turn to testify. She wept the whole time as she told about how she had met the young man at the river, and what had happened since. She showed the court the empty chest and described how it had been filled with gold coins. And she also took a vow that she had had no idea she was marrying a demon, for never, ever, would she do such a thing.

Then it was the turn of the river demon. He came forth, and all agreed that his presence was powerful, and that he was exceptionally handsome. And the river demon said: "Remember that Yona came to me in the first place by coming down to the river at night, for at that time the river belongs to the demons. So too did she freely accept the gifts with which we were betrothed, the gold coins and the bracelet I gave her at the time I spoke the words of the marriage vow. And that is not all. As you know, she also shared the wedding cake with me. Therefore she is my wife, and I insist on taking her back with me to the Kingdom of Demons."

Then the court of rabbis went off to decide the matter. It took them three hours to reach a decision. At last they said, "It is true that the trappings of a wedding did take place, but it is also true that it is forbidden for humans and demons to wed. Further, Yona was already engaged to someone else, and in the eyes of the law, an engagement is

the same as a marriage. Therefore the marriage to the demon is hereby revoked, and her marriage to her fiancé must take place by tomorrow. As for you, demon, as punishment, you must replace all the gold that disappeared from the chest of her dowry with real gold. If you do not, we will expel you to the driest desert on the face of the earth, where you will never see a river again!" When this judgment was announced, the river demon let out a shriek and vanished from their sight. But when they opened the chest, they saw it that it overflowing with gold coins—real ones—that were worth a fortune.

Yona returned home with her parents that night, and as soon as she walked through the door, she took off the bracelet the demon had given her and flung it into the fireplace, where it went up in smoke. And the next day, the wedding that Yona had longed for took place at last, and she and her groom had a long and happy life together, freed at last from the shadow of the river demon.

After the trial, the story of Yona was widely told, and all who heard it were forewarned not to go down to the river at night, when the river demons hold sway.

THE BALKANS: ORAL TRADITION

8. The Demonic Double

Once upon a time there was an orphan named Yusef, who lived alone in a hut at the edge of a forest. Every day he went out to gather branches to sell in the neighboring village. With the few pennies he earned, he was barely able to get by.

One day, when Yusef was looking for new sources of firewood, he walked into a part of the forest where he had never been before. By the time he realized how far he had gone, it was too late to get back home before night fell. Yusef knew it was not a good idea to spend the night in the forest, but since he had no choice, he decided to climb a tree, so that he would be safe from wild animals.

He looked up and saw a sturdy branch that looked as if it could safely hold him. He climbed up on that branch just before night fell. Soon the forest was pitch-black. Not even the moon could be seen.

Now, Yusef had no intention of sleeping that night. If he did, he might fall out of the tree. But he didn't have to worry about falling asleep. He was so frightened, he could depend on the sound of his heartbeat to keep him awake. He listened intently to all the sounds of the dark forest, trying to imagine what they were—was that a wolf howling or merely a dog?

Suddenly Yusef heard a voice saying, "Water, water." Yusef was so startled that he almost slipped off the branch. Whose voice was that? Now Yusef really started to worry. What kind of evil forces might make their home in such a forest?

Again he heard the voice crying out for water. This time Yusef recognized that it was a woman's voice. He shivered and peered around him, but he saw nothing in the darkness.

"Who are you?" Yusef whispered into the dark.

"My name is Devora. I was trapped inside a stone by a demoness who cast an evil spell. Tell me," the voice said, "did you bring any water with you?"

Now, Yusef was carrying water in a leather sack. "Yes," he said. "I have water. But where are you?"

"The trunk of this tree is hollow. Inside the trunk is a round stone. Pour water on that stone, and you will set me free."

Yusef had heard many stories about strange creatures inhabiting that forest. And he was afraid that this might be one of them. Maybe a demon was trying to trick him into setting it free. Then what would happen? In any case, he could do nothing till morning, when he could find the stone. Yusef decided to keep talking to the voice, to figure out if it was a demon or not.

So Yusef said, "How did you come to be trapped inside a stone?"

"My story is truly terrible," Devora replied. "I was trapped in a stone by a demon who is my double. She looks exactly like me, like my mirror image come to life. She cast her spell while I was on the way to my own wedding. Then she took my place as a bride, but no one knows anything about it. Even my groom does not know that he is married to a demon."

"How long have you been imprisoned inside the stone?" asked Yusef.

"I'm afraid I have lost track of time. Tell me, what year is this?"

When he told her, she said, "That means that three years have passed. For three years I have been trapped inside this terrible stone."

Yusef's eyes filled with tears. "That is the saddest story I've ever heard. I never knew such a thing was possible. Did you?"

"I should have listened to my grandmother," said Devora. "She was a midwife, and she told me that when every child is born, a double is born in the Kingdom of Demons. That double has his or her precise shape and image. This double waits until the person is about to get married, then finds a way trick the bride or groom into marrying the double instead. But I never thought it would happen to me. Now you are my only hope to be freed from this stone."

"How did the stone end up here?" Yusef asked.

"The demoness carried the stone to this remote place so that no one would find it and set me free. That is why you are my only hope. But tell me, who are you?"

"I'm Yusef," the boy said. "I lost my way in the forest and had to spend the night here."

"Surely it was destiny that you chose this tree," she said.

So it was that Yusef spoke to the voice all night long, until he was convinced that everything she said was true. He asked her to tell him how to set her free, and she told him exactly what to do.

Now, that was the longest night of Yusef's life. He felt that he had been stranded in a strange world, one where demons could trap people in stones and take their places. In a world where he had to be very careful, or he could end up trapped inside a stone himself.

When the sun finally rose, Yusef breathed a sigh of relief and climbed down to the ground. He saw that the trunk of the tree was hollow, and inside was a round stone, exactly where the voice had said it would be. Yusef hesitated before touching it, but he knew he could not leave that young woman trapped without hope. So he reached in and pulled out the stone, as swiftly and bravely as he could, and he quickly placed it on the ground and poured a few drops of water on it, as the voice had told him.

No sooner had the water touched the stone than Yusef heard a voice saying, "Oh, thank you!" And standing there before him was a beautiful young woman, dressed like a bride. She had dark eyes and long, flowing hair. And when Yusef saw her wearing her wedding gown, he knew that everything she had told him was true.

Yusef's heart went out to the young woman who had suffered so much on her day of joy, and he said, "Is there any way you can get your husband back?"

"Yes," said Devora. "I must defeat that demon and reclaim my life."

"How will you do that?" Yusef asked.

"I need your help," she said. "There is only one way for me to defeat that demoness. I must trap her with the same stone she used to imprison me. But I must never touch that stone again, or I will be trapped inside it forever. So I need your help, Yusef, in carrying the stone. But know that I will somehow repay you for your efforts."

Yusef picked up the stone that had been her prison and turned it over in his hands. It was as round as an orange, and about the same size. But even though it appeared to be ordinary, he knew that it was not.

"This demoness sounds as if she has great powers," said Yusef. "How can you possibly defeat her?"

"I know a few secrets myself," said Devora. "While I was trapped inside the stone, I found I could overhear everything that was said around me. For there are invisible creatures everywhere—angels, spirits, and demons. All of them whisper among themselves far too quietly for the living to hear. But inside that stone I heard every word they spoke, and I learned a great many secrets. Then my only hope was to escape from that stone. Now that I have, I must find a way to outwit my own double. But tell me, Yusef, will you help me?"

"Yes," Yusef said, "I will."

"Then let us set out at once for my village," said Devora, "where the demoness who has taken my place lives with the man who was destined to be my groom."

So Yusef and Devora set forth, with Devora leading the way. It was a strange sight to see a woman in a wedding gown walking in the forest. And Yusef thought that the world had completely changed overnight. It was far more dangerous than he had ever imagined, yet he was unafraid, perhaps because he wanted to help Devora, perhaps because she had survived without her spirit being broken. He was ready to accompany her until she had been restored to her rightful place.

Devora's village was many miles away, and as they walked together, Yusef and Devora devised a plan to defeat the demon who had stolen her life. When they reached the village, Devora remained hidden while Yusef went to the market and purchased a sack of big, beautiful oranges. Then Yusef went to the street where the demoness lived with the one who was supposed to have been Devora's husband. He called out, "Oranges for sale, oranges for sale." As he had hoped, the demoness came out to buy some. When Yusef saw her, he was amazed, for she was the very image of Devora, except that there was a wicked look in her eyes.

"Give me your three biggest oranges," the demoness said.

"As you wish," said Yusef. And he picked out one of the largest oranges and handed it to her. Then he picked out another and handed that to her as well.

"Don't you have any larger than that?" the demoness demanded.

"I will look," said Yusef. And he dug down deeply in the sack and said, "Yes, I have found a good one." At that instant, he pulled out the enchanted stone and thrust it into the hand of the demoness, who screamed when she saw it, but it was too late. All at once she vanished completely, leaving only a necklace behind. But Yusef and Devora knew exactly where she was. The moment the demoness touched the stone, she became trapped inside it.

Devora said, "Yusef, I will be grateful to you for the rest of my life. But now, to be safe, let us drop that stone into an abandoned well, so the demoness never finds a way to get out." So Yusef and Devora cast the cursed stone into the bottom of an old well that was dry as a bone, and that was the last they ever saw of it.

Then they returned to the house of Devora's fiancé, who had unwittingly married her demonic double. Even though Devora knew that she could probably take the place of the demon, since they were identical, she knew this was not right.

So when her fiancé came back home, she and Yusef told him her

story. At first he found it hard to believe, but when he saw that Devora was the mirror image of his wife, and far kinder, he finally realized that they were telling the truth. They decided to be secretly married, since they had never had a chance to say their vows. After their wedding, they adopted Yusef as their son, and they all lived happily ever after.

EASTERN EUROPE: ORAL TRADITION

9. Escape from the Kingdom of Demons

Once, while traveling on a ship, a merchant overheard two sailors telling tales about a famous witch. One was saying to the other, "There is nothing she can't accomplish with her spells." Now, the merchant had no children. He and his wife had tried every remedy without success. He wondered if the witch could help them, so he asked the sailors where she could be found. And when the ship arrived at the port of that city, he paid her a visit.

The merchant found the witch living in a little hut that looked as if it were about to collapse. But when he stepped inside, he found himself in a magnificent palace. Then he understood that the witch's powers were very great indeed.

As for the witch, she wasted no time. "I can see that you are searching for a child of your own," she said.

The merchant was speechless. He had not said anything, yet the witch knew exactly why he had come there.

"You want me to cast a spell," the witch said, "but the price is steep."

"I will pay it," the merchant said.

"Know, then," said the witch, "that your son will be born before the year is out, and he will be healthy in every respect. But heed my warning—see that he never sets foot on a ship. If he does, his fate will be in the hands of the demons!"

The merchant had not expected such a strange warning, and it worried him. Still, he assured the witch that he would do as she said, and after paying her, he left.

When the merchant returned to his own land, he told his wife about meeting the witch. She, too, was concerned about the witch's warning, but mostly she wondered if the spell would work. And, indeed, it did. That very year the merchant's wife gave birth to a beautiful son, whom they named Jared. They raised him well and saw that he was taught the Torah. But they never said anything to him about the dangers of ships. They didn't want to worry the boy. They would tell him when he grew older.

One day a ship came into port. The ship was carrying cargo belonging to the wealthy merchant, and the captain, who was an imposing figure, came to visit them. When he left, the boy said, "One day I, too, would like to be a ship's captain."

Now, that was the last thing the merchant and his wife wanted. And that night, when they were discussing whether or not to warn him about setting foot on a ship, Jared overheard them. He could not understand what they were worried about, and he decided to go down to the dock before he was forbidden to do so.

The next morning he hurried to the waterfront. And there was the captain's ship, moored close by. When no one was looking, Jared ran up the plank onto the deck.

He went down below, for he had always been curious to see a ship for himself. He climbed over trunks and barrels, exploring every corner of the hold. When he found a stack of soft rugs, he lay down, closed his eyes, and imagined that he was the captain, sailing to faraway lands. Before he knew it, he had fallen asleep.

When Jared awoke, he was surprised to find that the ship was rocking and waves were splashing against it. He ran to a porthole and saw that the ship had set out to sea. Fear swept over him, for stowaways were not treated kindly. Jared decided to stay hidden, for he didn't know what else to do.

Back home, Jared's parents began to worry. But no matter how much they searched, they couldn't find him.

Jared hid for days, sustained by a box of fresh fruit stored in the hold. But finally a sailor found him there and dragged him to the captain.

Now, that was of course the very captain who had visited the merchant's home, and he recognized Jared at once. Jared told him that he had only wanted to see what a ship was like, and that he had had no intention of being a stowaway. The captain believed him but explained that it was too late to turn back. He promised that as soon as the ship came into a port, Jared would be returned to his own land.

After that, Jared was permitted to wander wherever he wanted on the ship. The sailors taught him all about sailing and let him serve as a lookout. But when they had been at sea for only a week, a great storm struck. The ship tossed from side to side. Thunder roared. And suddenly a bolt of lightning struck the ship and split it apart. The captain ran to find Jared so he could take him to one of the lifeboats, but before he could reach him, the young stowaway was cast overboard. "Grab hold of a plank," the captain called out to Jared. And just before a great wave carried him away, he did. For three days and three nights, Jared was tossed by the waves as he clung to the plank with all his strength. But he was exhausted and losing his grip when suddenly a huge wave washed him onto the shore of a small island.

Jared collapsed on the sand and slept, but then hunger and thirst awakened him, and he began to explore the island. He found berries and fresh water there, and he ate and drank to his heart's content.

When Jared finished eating, he was surprised to see rabbits and deer racing past. Then he heard a great roar and realized that he, too, was in danger. He wanted to run away, but the roaring was so close that he had to scramble up the nearest tree, frantically pulling himself into the highest branches.

When he looked down, Jared saw a fierce lion standing on its hind legs, clawing the tree trunk and baring its huge teeth.

Suddenly the tree began to sway in the wind, and Jared clutched the branches, afraid he would fall into the jaws of the lion. He looked up and saw that the tree was being fanned by the wings of a giant ziz, the most enormous bird he had ever seen. And before he knew what was happening, that giant bird had snatched Jared with its talons and flown off toward a distant land. Completely terrified, Jared looked down and saw the ocean far below and prayed he would not fall from that great height.

Before long, the ziz had crossed the ocean and was flying low over a forest. As it did, the ziz dropped the boy, and he went tumbling down, landing in the top of a tree that broke his fall. For a long time he lay sprawled on a limb, still shaking after the terrifying ride.

When Jared finally climbed down to the ground, his legs trembled so much, he could barely stand. He sat down, leaning against the trunk of a tree, trying to think. How could he find his way out of that forest before nightfall? There was no sign of a path, but there were birds flying overhead—and they were all flying in the same direction. So Jared decided to follow them.

Late that afternoon, Jared emerged from the forest and saw a town in the distance. He wondered what town it was and what land he was in. Would anyone there even speak his language? But he was hungry and thirsty, so he had no other choice but to seek help.

When Jared reached the town, he heard music and followed the sound until he came to a brightly lit mansion. He peered through a window and saw that a wedding celebration was taking place. An enormous crowd was dancing wildly past tables laden with great stacks of mouth-watering food.

Jared was so famished, he decided to try to get some of that food, even at the risk of being caught. So he climbed through the window and filled his pockets with pitas and fresh fruit. Just then a girl wearing a silver crown grabbed Jared by the arm. "You can always eat later," she said. "Let's dance." And she made him join the circle of dancers.

Never had Jared whirled so fast in his life. He was becoming dizzy when suddenly the dancing stopped. A soldier was ringing a bell, and everyone wanted to hear what he had to say.

"Know that we have found the footprints of a human being under the window," the soldier said. "And we have come to search for the intruder. Tell us if you see him."

Everyone at the wedding began to shout and look around, for human beings were strictly forbidden in that land. Jared's heart sank, because he knew those footprints were his. The girl with the silver crown was his only hope. He whispered in her ear, "Quickly, you must hide me." She looked at him with surprise, but then she took his hand and led him out of the room.

"Who are you?" she asked.

"I'm Jared. I came here by accident. I mean no harm. Please help me."

"Then follow me. My name is Ifrit."

She led Jared through many rooms and out a side door of the mansion. They hurried through the winding streets of the city until they reached a palace that dwarfed the mansion they had left behind. As they approached the palace gates, Jared hesitated. There were guards standing there.

"Don't be afraid," Ifrit said. "The guards would never question anyone who is with me—for I am the princess."

They strolled through the gates, and the guards bowed low as they passed by.

"Then it's true!" said Jared. "You *are* the princess, and that's a real crown."

"Certainly," said Ifrit, "and that's why I can hide you. This is the palace of my father, Ashmodai, the King of Demons. The watchman has three hundred and sixty-four keys for the three hundred and sixty-four rooms he checks every day. But he has no key to the three hundred and sixty-fifth room. That is my room. I am the only one allowed to enter it, and I can safely hide you there."

Jared could barely believe that a princess was trying to save him. She unlocked her bedroom door and led him into a huge closet. Then she gave him food and water and said she must return to the wedding before she was missed.

"Wait," said Jared. "Please tell me what country this is."

"Why, this is the Kingdom of Demons," said Ifrit. "Didn't you know? Didn't you know that no humans are allowed to enter, on penalty of death? You are in grave danger."

"Then I must escape," said Jared. "But why are you being so kind to me if humans are so hated here?"

"You are the first human I have ever met," she said. "And you seem nice enough to me." Then she hurried back to the wedding.

Jared ate some of the food the princess had given him and slept until she returned late that night.

"Soldiers are still searching for you everywhere," she said. "They are watching the border day and night. But luckily I know a secret that my father once told me."

"What is it?" begged Jared.

"There is a hidden cave that leads directly from this kingdom to the land of the humans. Neither humans nor demons know anything about it. It is a secret passed down in our family. My father once showed me where it is. But we can't make our way to that cave now, because everyone is on the lookout for you—unless . . ."

"Unless what?"

"Unless we cover you with the cloak of invisibility," said the princess. "You see, my father, Ashmodai, has a trunk filled with magical items. Among them is a cloak that makes you invisible. There also is a magic map in that trunk that always tells you where you are, and a gold purse that is never empty. But these things are very precious to my father. That's why he wears the key to that chest around his neck. How would I ever be able to get it?"

Jared realized that her father would be very angry if he caught her trying to steal the key. He told her not to risk angering her father for him.

"I'm afraid there's no choice," she said. "I'll have to steal it to save your life."

That very night the princess crept into her father's room and took the key from around his neck while he was sleeping. Then she quietly opened the chest and took out the cloak of invisibility, quickly putting it on. She also took out the map and the purse. After closing the chest and locking it, she carefully put the key back, all without waking her father.

Still invisible, she came back and stood by the chair where Jared was sitting.

"Here I am," Ifrit said.

Poor Jared was so frightened that he almost fell onto the floor. He heard a demonic giggle and then saw the princess emerge from under the cloak.

"I couldn't resist," Ifrit said. "Hurry. Put this on."

So Jared slipped the cloak of invisibility over his head. He was amazed to find that he could no longer see his hands or feet. He was as invisible as Ifrit had been a moment before.

"You must go alone," she said. "If anyone saw me leaving in the middle of the night, they would awaken my father. But this map will help you. I marked the place where the secret cave can be found. The map will show you when you are getting closer, guiding the way. And take this purse. It will always serve you well."

Jared was speechless. The demon princess had been so kind to him. He owed his life to her. What could he say?

"I will never forget you," Jared said at last. "I will always be grateful."

"Go quickly now," said the princess, and she led him to the front hall of the palace.

She told the guard she wanted some fresh air. So the guard opened the door, and the princess stepped outside. Jared did too, although the guard never knew it. The last thing the princess whispered in his ear was "Good luck!" Then Jared hurried down the path, the magic map in his hand.

He was still in danger, but he felt far safer with the cloak making him invisible and the map leading the way. Indeed, there was a glowing light on that wonderful map that let him know where he was. And when he finally found the cave, the map lit up the darkness.

When Jared emerged from the cave, he found himself standing in the very forest that was outside his own town. He ran home so fast, he almost flew. And only when he reached his house did he remember that he was still wearing the cloak of invisibility. Imagine how surprised his parents were when he pulled it off!

Now, when Jared's parents recovered from the shock of his unexpected return, he told them about his adventures from the time he had explored the ship. His parents could hardly believe that such things could happen—until he showed them the cloak of invisibility, the magic map, and the magic purse. When they saw these wonderful things, they knew that everything he had told them was true. They wept and said, "It's all our fault. If only we had warned you that you were not to set foot on a ship!"

"I must confess that I heard you talking about that," Jared said. "That is why I boarded the ship. I was very curious. If only I had known what awaited me!"

Then Jared opened the magic purse and pulled out a gold coin. But the purse was as heavy as it had been a moment before, because another coin had replaced the one he took out.

Jared looked at the coin. On the front was the portrait of Ashmodai, the King of Demons, who looked terribly fierce. Jared was grateful that they had never met. And on the back was a portrait of the demon princess, Ifrit.

Jared's parents were amazed when they saw her portrait, for it made them realize that even among demons, there were some who were kindly.

As for Jared, he carried one of those gold coins with him wherever he went. And he never forgot his friend the demon princess.

NORTH AFRICA: THIRTEENTH CENTURY

Sources

I. The Kingdom of Angels

1. The Angel's Gift (Poland)

   Based on IFA 4591, collected by Itshak Veksler from Mr. Talshir, and IFA 14728, collected by Yardena Hazor from Zohara Algrabali of Morocco.

2. The Angel's Sword (Babylon)

   From the Babylonian Talmud, tractate Ketubot 77b.

3. The Angel's Daughter (Bukhara)

   From *Asarah Sipurei am mi Bukharah* (Hebrew), edited by Dov Noy. IFA 7705, collected by Ya' akov Pinhasi. Jerusalem: Israel Folktale Archives, 1978. AT 400–424, AT 759, and AT 934C. This story finds its origin in the story of the scapegoat in the Bible, who is sent to Azazel (Leviticus 16:8–10).

II. The Kingdom of Spirits

4. A Roomful of Ghosts (Eastern Europe)

   From *Sipurei Hasidim*, edited by Shlomo Yosef Zevin (Tel Aviv: 1956–57), and from *Nishmat Yisrael*, edited by Yisroel Ya'akov Klapholtz. (B'nai Brak: 1989).

5. King David Is Alive (Poland)

   IFA 966, collected by Nehama Zion from Miriam Tschernobilski of Poland.

6. The Lost Melody (Germany)

   From *Me-Otsar Genazai* by Hayim Dov Armon Kastenbaum, edited by Alter Ze'ev Wortheim (Tel Aviv: 1932). From the memory of Hayim Dov Armon Kastenbaum, who heard this story from his grandmother.

III. The Kingdom of Demons

7. Yona and the River Demon (The Balkans)

   From *Sipurei am, Romanssot, ve'Orebot-bayim shel Yehudei Sefard* by Max Grunwald, tale no. 50, edited by Dov Noy (Jerusalem: 1982). Folklore Research Center Studies VI. Collected by Max Grunwald from an unknown teller from the Balkans.

8. The Demonic Double (Eastern Europe)

   IFA 12379, collected by Dvora Vilk from Juliet Ya'akovlaba, who heard the story from her mother, Ada Kavka, born in Baku, Caucas.

9. Escape from the Kingdom of Demons (North Africa)

   From *Ma'aseh Yerushalmi*, edited by Yehudah L. Zlotnik (Jerusalem: 1946). First published in Constantinople in the sixteenth century. Legend holds that this story was told by Abraham, the son of Maimonides, in the thirteenth century. A variant is found in *Sippurim: Prager Sammlung Jüdischer Legenden in Neuer Auswahl und Bearbeitung* (Vienna and Leipzig: 1921). An oral variant is IFA 8129, collected by Lili David from Rachel ha-Rambam of Persia.